and the
Terrible Talking Termite

THE Berenstain BEAR SCOUTS
and the
Terrible Talking Termite

by Stan & Jan Berenstain

Illustrated by Michael Berenstain

A
LITTLE APPLE
PAPERBACK

SCHOLASTIC INC.

New York Toronto London Auckland Sydney

ISBN 0-590-60383-3

Copyright © 1996 by Berenstain Enterprises, Inc. All rights reserved. Published by Scholastic Inc. APPLE PAPERBACKS and the APPLE PAPERBACKS logo are registered trademarks of Scholastic Inc.

12 11 10 9 8 7 6 5 4 3 2   6 7 8 9/9 0 1/0

Printed in the U.S.A.   40

First Scholastic printing, June 1996

• Table of Contents •

THE Berenstain BEAR SCOUTS

and the

Terrible Talking Termite

• Chapter 1 •
Crossing Paths

The "one for all, and all for one!" Bear Scouts were on their way to their secret chicken coop clubhouse. They were within sight of it when they saw a familiar figure in the distance.

"Look!" said Scout Brother. "Isn't that Ralph Ripoff cutting across Farmer Ben's pasture?"

"It looks like Ralph Ripoff," said Scout Fred.

"But," said Scout Sister, "he doesn't look the way Ralph usually looks." It was true. Even though Ralph was wearing his

usual snazzy clothes — green plaid suit, straw hat, and spats — he didn't look the way he usually looked. Ralph usually walked with a spring in his step, his head held high and his walking stick a-twirl. But not today. Today, he was shuffling along, staring at the ground, dragging his walking stick behind him.

A group of Farmer Ben's cows was grazing in Ralph's path.

"If he doesn't look where he's going, he's going to bump into Ben's cows," said Brother.

"They're not as mean as Ben's bull," said Sister. "But they won't stand for any nonsense." But Ralph didn't bump into the cows. They saw him coming and opened a path for him. He shuffled right through the cows without even seeing them. He just kept shuffling along, staring at the ground.

"Wow," said Scout Fred. "I've never seen Ralph looking so down."

"Right," said Scout Lizzy. "He's usually got a cheery grin, even when you catch him with his hand in the cookie jar."

"Something must have gone very wrong in Ralph's life," said Brother.

"Maybe some big crooked deal fell through and he got left holding the bag," said Fred.

"Maybe," said Brother. "But I don't think so."

"Maybe he tried to sell somebody a gold brick and the gold paint got scraped off," said Lizzy.

"Maybe," said Brother. "But I don't think so."

"Maybe he went to Dr. Gert for a checkup and she told him he only had twenty minutes to live," said Sister.

"I *hope* not," said Brother.

"Right," said Fred. "Ralph may be a miserable rotten low-down crook, but I'd sure miss him if he weren't around."

"Miss Ralph?" said Sister. "How come?"

"Well," said Fred, "I'd miss him because . . . well, it's kind of hard to explain."

As the scouts moved along the road, Ralph kept cutting across the pasture toward the woods that bordered Farmer Ben's farm. If they kept going, their paths would soon cross.

"I know what Fred means," said

Brother. "We've got Ralph to thank for some good adventures."

"You mean like the time we saved Giant Bat Cave when Ralph tried to turn it into an underground theme park?" said Lizzy.

"And it was Ralph," said Sister, "who

tricked Papa into planting that weird seed that grew into that humongous pumpkin."

Ralph was closer now. He was still shuffling, still staring at the ground.

"It's sort of like those mystery books that Fred's always reading," said Brother. "The ones about the famous detective and the master criminal."

"You mean Grizzlock Holmes and Professor Beariority?" said Fred. "I guess that's right. It's like Ralph is Professor Beariority and we're Grizzlock Holmes." Ralph was much closer now. "Look at him," said Fred. "He looks like he's lost his best friend."

"And since Ralph is his own best friend, that could be serious," said Sister. Ralph sure looked like a lost soul as he shuffled along. All that was needed to complete the picture was a cartoon gloom cloud over his head.

"Let's wait and ask him if he needs help

or something," said Brother. The scouts waited.

"What's the trouble, Ralph?" asked Brother as Beartown's leading crook and swindler crossed the road. "Is there anything we can do to help?" But the Bear Scouts may as well have been Farmer Ben's cows. Ralph didn't even see them as he headed toward the woods.

"He didn't even see us!" said Lizzy.

"Where do you suppose he's going?" said Sister.

"Home is where the heart is," said Brother. "So I guess he's headed for that houseboat of his."

"Boy, living in that smelly, broken-down old houseboat would be enough to make me gloomy," said Sister.

"Speaking of smelly," said Brother, "it's been a while since we touched base at the clubhouse. There's no telling how many chickens have dropped by and left 'souvenirs,' so let's get a move on." As the scouts came close to their clubhouse they saw another figure in the distance. This time, it was Farmer Ben. He was heading their way on the run.

"Scouts! Scouts!" he shouted. "I have a message for you! An urgent message!"

• Chapter 2 •

His Own Worst Enemy

The Bear Scouts were on to something when they talked about Ralph being his own best friend. The trouble was that he had gone from being his own best friend to being his own worst enemy. Somewhere along the line he'd lost the one thing a swindler must have: confidence. Ralph had lost faith in his ability to trick, cheat, and swindle. And it's fair to say, a swindler without confidence can be his own worst enemy.

Not even the simple swindles that were

his bread and butter were working. Ralph knew he was really in trouble when a tiny cub — a cub in arms, actually — guessed which shell the pea was under.

What's happening? he wondered. Have I lost my touch? Or is it just that folks are on to me? As for "big cons" — schemes that promised a pot of gold at the end of a crooked rainbow — Ralph couldn't *steal* an idea.

The sight of his houseboat used to cheer Ralph. But not anymore. It needed paint, the brass was green, and some of its planks were sprung. Was this the boat he had planned to turn into a gambling ship that would light up the river and make piles of money for Captain Ralph Ripoff? Hardly. Now it was just a rotting hulk moored in a smelly backwater.

"Permission to come aboard!" said Ralph as he neared the splintery gang-plank.

"Permission granted! Permission granted!" squawked Squawk, Ralph's pet parrot.

Ralph sighed as he slumped into his captain's chair. "Squawk, old buddy," he said, "I've got good news and bad news."

"Good news and bad news! Good news and bad news!" squawked Squawk.

"The good news is that Chief of Police Bruno doesn't chase me out of town anymore." Another sigh. "The bad news is that I haven't been able to cheat anybody out of their hard-earned money for weeks. The sad fact is that I've lost my touch. Suckers are catching me with cards up my sleeve. My two-headed coin trick doesn't even work anymore. I've got to face it, Squawk. It's over. I'm a crumbled cookie. I've gone brain-dead."

"Brain-dead! Brain-dead!" squawked Squawk.

"I used to spin off schemes like a Roman candle. Now, I'm just spinning my wheels. Nothing's happening, Squawk. Why, I haven't gotten a phone call in weeks. I don't even get mail anymore." Ralph looked across the houseboat at his

awards and trophies. They were given to
him by such groups as the Academy of
Crooks and Swindlers. He walked over to
the trophy shelf. He picked up a trophy.
"Listen to this, Squawk," he said. He read
the words that were inscribed on it.
"'Ralph Ripoff, Swindler of the Year!' Did
you hear that? *Swindler of the Year!*"

Another sigh. "What am I gonna do,
Squawk? What am I gonna do?"

Squawk was ready with an answer.
"Get an honest job! Get an honest job!" he
squawked.

"Bite your tongue, you nasty bird!" said Ralph.

"Honest job! Honest job!" insisted Squawk. Ralph went nose to beak with the parrot.

"I said bite your tongue," said Ralph, "or I'll bite it for you!" It was a good thing the phone rang at that moment. Ralph and Squawk had gone nose to beak before, and Ralph usually got the worst of it. "The phone!" he said. "I'll bet it's one of my old buddies, Crooked Cal or Sam Sleaze, calling for help on a big con! Things are looking up, Squawk!" But when Ralph reached the ringing phone and answered it, his face fell and the light went out of his eyes.

"Insurance? *Insurance?*" he said. "You're tying up my line to sell me insurance? Get off the phone, you . . ." He crashed the phone onto its cradle. Squawk had never seen Ralph so angry. "It's bad enough the chief doesn't chase me out of town anymore. Now, I'm on sucker lists! Me, the great Ralph Ripoff, on sucker lists! Oh, how the mighty have fallen." He slumped into his captain's chair. As he did so, he heard the "klunk" the postbear made when he raised the flag on Ralph's mailbox.

It was the first mail he'd gotten in days. But he wasn't about to get his hopes up the way he did when the phone rang. Most likely it was just bills. He rose and went down the gangplank. He lowered the flag and opened the mailbox. There was mail. But it wasn't just bills. His *Swindler Magazine* had come.

Ralph decided to look through it for ideas. He certainly could use some. "Hmm," he said as he looked at the ads. "Here's one, 'Make Big Money with Miracle Hair-Grow! An Amazing New Product That Can Grow Hair on Billiard Balls!' Forget it. Who needs hairy billiard balls?" Ralph read on. "Hmm. Here's another one about hair, 'Send Twenty Dollars and We'll Tell You How to Avoid Falling Hair.' I know the answer to that one: Jump out of the way."

Ralph didn't really have much hope of finding a good idea in the magazine. But as he stood there leafing through it, a very weird thing happened. Somebody or something said, "Hi, there!" in a small but very clear voice. Ralph did a quick, startled scan of the area. But there was no one to be seen.

"I'm down here!" said the voice. Ralph looked down. What he saw was so weird and frightening that he would have jumped into his own arms if he'd known how.

There, standing on a rock at the base of the post that held up the mailbox, was an enormous bug! Ralph tried to speak. But he'd lost his voice. When he found it, all he could do was stutter, "Wh-wh-what in the S-S-Sam Hill are you?"

"Sam Hill has nothing to do with it. But it's a reasonable question. And since I *am* a bit hungry, I'll show you." With that, the giant bug scurried over to a log and ate it. There was a noise like a buzz saw, and before you could say Terrible Talking Termite, the log had turned into a pile of sawdust.

"Y-y-you're a termite," said Ralph.

"I am indeed," said the creature. "Woody's my name, and mine is a strange and sad story. Would you like to hear it?"

"I'm all ears," said Ralph. He was not only all ears, he was atwitter with excitement as well. He was putting together that phone call about insurance with this amazing buzz saw of a giant termite. A combination of the two might be just what he was looking for: a really big con.

• Chapter 3 •

A Cry for Help

"Did Professor Actual Factual say what the problem was — what he wants to see us about?" said Brother.

"Nope," said Farmer Ben. "Mrs. Ben took the phone message, and here it is." He unfolded the message and read, "'Please tell the Bear Scouts that I need help. They are to come to the Bearsonian ASAP!' Whatever that means."

"It means 'As Soon as Possible!'" said Fred.

"Yeah," said Farmer Ben, scratching his

head. "I guess it does at that." He handed the message to Brother.

"Was this the whole message?" said Brother.

"That was it," said Ben. "Well, got things to do. Gotta get my cows in for milkin'." Ben trotted off in the direction of his barn. "Yo, Bossy! Yo, Bossy!" he called. The cows stopped munching grass and slowly followed.

"Well, what do you think?" said Fred.

"I think we have to head over to the Bearsonian ASAP," said Brother.

"I guess so," said Fred. "But what about the clubhouse? It probably needs a good cleaning. And we're supposed to decide about our next merit badge."

"Those things can wait," said Brother. "Actual Factual has called for help. It's up to us to answer his call."

"Then let's stop talking about it," said

Sister, "and *do it!*" With that, Sister headed back down the road on the run. The rest of the troop followed.

The professor's call for help sounded pretty urgent. So the scouts took a short-cut across one of Ben's plowed fields. It was a little mushy, but they made good time by running between the furrows. By the time the Bearsonian came into view, they were out of breath. They slowed to a walk.

"Everything looks normal at the Bear-sonian," said Fred.

"We didn't exactly figure it was on fire or had collapsed," said Lizzy. It would have taken a lot to collapse the Bearson-ian. It was a huge stone building that had been built to last. Its full and proper name was The Bearsonian Museum of Science and Nature. It had a Hall of Prehistory, a Hall of Plants and Animals, and a Hall of

Energy. Fred was heavily into dinosaurs.
So, of course, the Hall of Prehistory was
his favorite. Lizzy had a special feeling for
nature. So, naturally, her favorite was the
Hall of Plants and Animals. Sister, who
was a bundle of energy, liked the Hall of
Energy with its tesla coil that made lightning when you cranked the handle. What
Brother liked most about the Bearsonian
was Professor Actual Factual himself. Actual Factual was not only a great scientist
but a great friend as well.

There hadn't been any question about
answering the professor's call for help.
But there was a lot of curiosity about what
the problem was. As the scouts came
closer to the great looming building, their
curiosity grew.

• Chapter 4 •

The Case of the Empty Cases

There was a big poster on display in front of the museum. It said:

OPENING SOON!

EXCITING NEW EXHIBIT!

A STUDY OF MUTATION IN DROSOPHILI!

"Droso — *what?*" said Sister.

"It's over *my* head," said Lizzy.

"It's Greek to me," said Brother. "Fred, you're the one who reads the dictionary just for fun. You figure it out."

"Actually, it's Latin," said Fred. "And I haven't gotten around to the Latin dictionary yet."

"As I live and breathe! It's the Bear Scouts! What are you doing here?" It was Professor Actual Factual. He was standing on the museum's front steps.

"You sent for us, Professor," said Brother. "Look. Here's your message." He handed the note to Actual Factual.

"So I did. So I did," said the professor. "In any case, welcome to the Bearsonian!" That's the way the professor was. He often forgot things. It wasn't that he was absentminded. It was just that he was so smart that sometimes his brain overpowered his memory.

31

Brother lagged behind as the professor led the scouts up the front steps into the museum. He was still wondering what the professor's call for help was about. He took a quick look around. There weren't any broken windows, and there wasn't any graffiti on the walls.

The new exhibit was just inside the front door.

"Well," said the professor. "What do you think of my new exhibit?" His new study was set up on a long table. What it looked like was a row of empty glass cases. The only hint that maybe they weren't empty was a big magnifying glass lying on the table beside the first case. A sign repeated what it said on the poster, "A STUDY OF MUTATION IN DROSOPHILI!" The scouts looked at the empty glass cases. They looked hard.

"Do you see anything?" said Brother under his breath.

"Nope," said Fred. "How about you, Sister?"

"Nope," said Sister. But Lizzy, who was famous for her sharp eyesight, thought she saw something. She picked up the magnifying glass.

"Well," said the professor, "what do you think of it?"

"Frankly, professor," said Brother, "we don't know *what* to think."

"Oh, dear," said the professor. "That's what I was afraid of." He slumped onto a stool beside the exhibit. He looked very discouraged.

• Chapter 5 •

Nature's Great Plan

"Professor," said Sister, who was the most outspoken of the scouts. "What are we *supposed* to think about empty glass cases? And, besides, what the heck are droso — whatchamacallits?"

"Of course, the cases aren't empty. And drosophili — pronounced dro-*sof*-i-lee — are fruit flies."

"You mean those nasty little things that hang around fruit?" said Sister.

"They're not nasty!" said Lizzy, who was still looking through the magnifying glass. She put it down and went head to head with Sister. "They're part of Nature's Great Plan, and there's no need to insult them!"

"Oh, yeah?" said Sister. "What do you hear from your friends, the cockroaches, the slugs, and the dung beetles?"

Lizzy and Sister were best friends. But even best friends have arguments sometimes.

"Now, now," said the professor. "I don't like to take sides, but Lizzy does have a point. All those creatures *are* part of Nature's Great Plan."

"Hey!" said Fred, who had followed Lizzy's lead and was studying the fruit flies through the magnifying glass. "I get it! These are mutations! The ones in the second case are different from the ones in the first case. They have different-shaped wings. And the ones in the third case have purple eyes. And the ones in the . . ."

"Fred," said the professor. "Perhaps you would favor us with a definition of 'mutation.'"

"*Mutation*," said Fred. "Pronounced *myoo-tay-shun; the process of change, especially in life-forms.*"

"Exactly," said the professor. "Mutations, too, are part of Nature's Great Plan, a very important part. You see, the fruit fly's very short life cycle has allowed me to

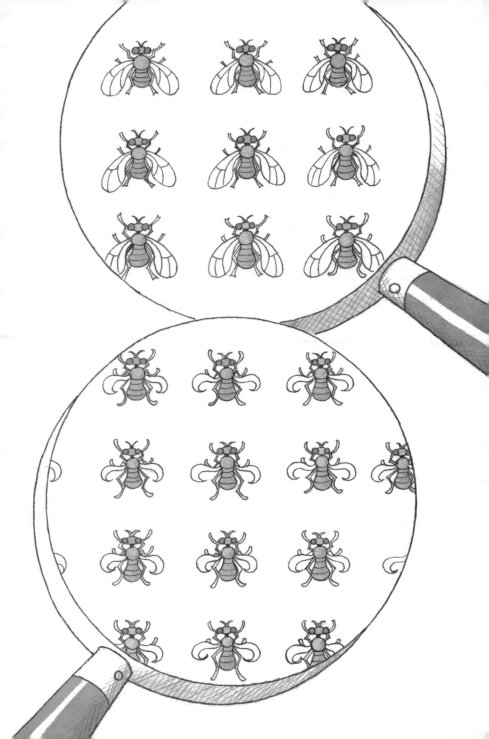

show how rapidly life-forms can change."

"I guess it's pretty interesting, Professor," said Brother. "But what's so important about it?"

"Isn't it obvious?" said the professor. (Of course, it wasn't.) "Understanding mutation is very important in fighting disease. Many kinds of germs have learned to change and 'outsmart' the medicines doctors use."

"Yes," said Fred, who kept up on science. "I've heard about that — how some medicines sort of stop working."

"And it's very important in farming, too," said Actual Factual. "Many pests that destroy crops have changed and 'outsmarted' the methods farmers use to protect their crops."

"That's right," said Brother. "I heard Farmer Ben telling Papa about how the bug stuff he uses doesn't work on the corn worm anymore."

"But, alas," said the professor, "the great importance of my study was completely lost on Squire Grizzly."

"Squire Grizzly?" asked Brother. "What's he got to do with it?"

"A great deal," said the professor. "He's head of the museum's board of governors. It's the board that gives us our money — including the money for this study."

"What did the squire think of the study?" asked Brother.

"Not very much, I'm afraid," said the professor. "He's not as sharp-eyed as you cubs. He couldn't see the fruit flies even with the magnifying glass. When I tried to explain it to him he just growled. But that wasn't the worst of it. He took a quick tour of the museum. He wasn't pleased. I can't say that I blame him. I must admit that I've become so wrapped up in my scientific studies that I may have let the museum run down a bit."

A *bit*? thought the scouts as they looked around. It looked to them like the professor had let the museum run down a *lot*. There was dust everywhere. The museum souvenir shop was all cobwebby and had a "closed" sign on the door. There was even a pile of fossil bones in one corner. And that was just what they could see from the lobby.

"So what finally happened with the squire?" said Brother.

"He took another look at the lobby, growled a few more times," said the professor, "then he said I'd hear from him and stormed out muttering under his breath." The professor just looked off into space for a moment. Then he reached into his jacket pocket and took out a letter. "I got this letter this morning," he said. "That's why I sent for you." He handed the letter to Brother. Brother read it aloud.

My Dear Professor,

This is to tell you that I shall strongly advise the board to stop providing money to the Bearsonian. The board will vote on the matter at the end of the month.

Yours truly,
Squire Grizzly
Chairbear

P.S. I plan to make one more visit to the museum before the next board meeting.

There was no question about it. The professor and the Bearsonian were in big trouble.

• Chapter 6 •

Only Ralph Knows
Wood So Good!

"I'm just a sport of nature, I suppose," said the giant talking bug.

"Just a *freak* of nature," said Ralph under his breath. When he first saw the enormous termite, he felt like a character in a horror movie. But now that he was over the shock, he was beginning to see the weird creature as the chance for a comeback.

Thank goodness for that call about insurance, he thought. If not for that, he might never have gotten the idea that was now forming in the maze of his twisted mind. Termites and insurance. Perfect together!

Ralph had heard of some weird and amazing things in his time. Some of the circuses and carnivals where he had worked — mostly as a pickpocket — had freak shows. So he had seen some pretty weird things, too. But most of them were fakes or tricks. Jo-Jo, The Dog-faced Bear, for example, was a bear with special makeup and false bloodhound ears. Tessa, The Talking Head, of course, was a trick done with mirrors. But Woody, The Talking Termite, was neither a fake nor a trick done with mirrors. Woody was the genuine article: a trick of nature.

And speaking of tricks, Ralph could hardly wait to try his termite insurance scheme on some real-live suckers. Especially his favorite sucker, Papa Q. Bear. Just the thought of tricking Papa into

WOODY, THE TALKING TERMITE

buying termite insurance made Ralph feel
warm all over.

Here's how it would work: Ralph would
offer to sell somebody termite insurance.
Since termites weren't a big problem
around Beartown, the offer would be re-
fused. Ralph would politely take "no" for
an answer and leave. Then, from a safe
distance, he would turn his secret weapon
loose on the sucker's home sweet home.
Sawdust would fly, and the homeowner

would beg to buy Ralph's insurance. Of course, the price would have doubled by then. Then Ralph would retrieve Woody by means of a fine nylon fishing line (termites can't eat nylon). He would put him back in his little tin box (they can't eat metal, either) and be on his merry way.

It was foolproof. It couldn't miss. And the money he would make! It might even be enough to restart his dream of turning his houseboat into a gambling ship. All it would take was a little paint, some new brightwork, and some crooked gambling machines. Oh, joy! All things were possible with a really big con!

But even the sweetest swindle has its downside. The fact was that Ralph didn't even like ordinary bugs. As for this giant monster of a bug, just thinking about him gave Ralph the galloping creepy crawlies. Being nice to Woody was going to take some doing. But there was a lot at stake. So Ralph gritted his teeth and did it.

When Woody told Ralph the sad story of how he was kicked out of the nest, Ralph tsk-tsked in a kindly manner.

"I really can't blame them," said Woody. "I was so big, you see."

"Yes," said Ralph. "I see." When Woody was hungry, Ralph brought him snacks of twigs and branches.

"What's that big thing in the water?" said Woody. "It looks delicious."

"That's my houseboat," said Ralph, a little nervously. "I live there. And, of course," he added, "friends don't eat each other's homes."

"You mean . . . we're *friends*?" said Woody.

"We're better than friends," said Ralph. "We're partners. We're going to work together."

"Oh, thank you, Ralph!" said Woody. "Thank you! Thank you! Thank you!" Woody was so grateful, he didn't even complain when Ralph shut him up in the mailbox.

"I hope you don't mind, partner," said Ralph as he closed Woody up in the mailbox with some twigs. "I just want to keep you safe."

"I don't mind," said Woody.

"Now I've got some things to do," said Ralph. "Just call me if you need me."

Ralph climbed the gangplank onto the houseboat. He sat at his desk with pen and paper.

"There's one born every minute! One born every minute!" squawked Squawk.

"Shh!" said Ralph. "I've got to concentrate. I've got to write me an insurance policy." He touched the handle of the pen to his chin and looked off into the distance for inspiration. Sure enough, it came. This is what he wrote: "Insurance by Ralph. Termite Insurance a Specialty. Only Ralph knows wood so good!"

Before very long, Ralph had the whole thing worked out. "There we are," he said. "As fine a phony insurance policy as I've ever seen. Right down to the dotted line for the suckers to sign on."

"Dotted line! Dotted line!" squawked the parrot.

"And now, my fine feathered friend," said Ralph, "I'm off to Herb's Quick Print!"

"Herb's Quick Print! Herb's Quick Print!" squawked Squawk.

• Chapter 7 •
Action Plan

"Would you excuse us, professor?" said Brother.

"You're not leaving?" asked Actual Factual.

"No," said Brother. "We just want to have a little meeting."

"Don't worry," said Sister. "It's a scout thing." The scouts walked across the lobby. They wanted to talk where the professor couldn't hear them. They headed for a small alcove that was used as a coatroom. At least, it was used as a coatroom when large numbers of visitors came to the

Bearsonian. All it had now was coat hangers.

"It looks to me," said Brother as the scouts gathered in the alcove, "like Actual Factual told it like it is. He's gotten so wrapped up in his science that he let the museum really fall apart."

"You've got that right," said Lizzy. "Half the lightbulbs are burned out and you could choke on the dust."

"The souvenir shop looks like the mummies' tomb," said Sister.

"I peeked into the Hall of Prehistory," said Fred. "And I'm sorry to say that the professor hasn't kept up on modern dinosaur theory."

"And that business with the fruit flies may be good science," said Sister, "but as an exhibit, it wouldn't pass show-and-tell."

"Just hold it, please," said Brother. "Let's not get hung up on details. We'll deal with those later. What we need is an action plan. I started thinking about one as soon as I came in the front door. Here it is. . . ."

Sister, Fred, and Lizzy listened hard as Brother laid out his plan for saving the Bearsonian.

"Well," said Fred, when Brother finished. "I think the cleanup, fix-up part of the plan is fine. But I don't know about closing the museum, then having a grand reopening."

"What is there to lose?" said Brother. "If we don't get the cleanup, fix-up part done before Squire Grizzly's next visit, the whole museum could shut down anyway."

"He's right," said Sister.

"Then, come on," Fred said. "Let's fill the professor in. There's no time to lose."

Actual Factual listened carefully to the scouts' action plan. "Well," he said when

they finished, "it's pretty ambitious. Do you really think we can bring it off?"

"Sure," said Brother. "With a little help from our friends."

"Correction," said Sister. "With a *lot* of help from our friends!"

"It's slogan time!" said Brother.

"What are we going to cross?" asked Fred.

"How about these fossil bones?" said the professor.

"Will you join us?" said Brother.

"Don't mind if I do," said the professor. So the fossil bones were crossed and the Bear Scouts' "One for all, and all for one!" slogan echoed through the dusty gloom. Now, all they had to do was put their action plan into action.

• Chapter 8 •

FOB for Short

"Now, let's see if I've got this straight," said Sister. The Bear Scouts had left the Bearsonian and were coming back across Farmer Ben's field. "The first thing we're gonna do to help Actual Factual out of the fix he's in is ask Grizzly Gus to put a crew together and clean up the Bearsonian, and the next thing . . ."

"No," said Brother. "The first thing we're gonna do is *raise money* so we can *hire* Grizzly Gus to put a crew together, and then . . ."

"Right," said Sister, "and we're gonna

raise money by going to Actual Factual's friends and begging for it."

"No!" said Fred. "We're going to give Actual Factual's friends the opportunity to help him by buying memberships in a great new organization called Friends of the Bearsonian — or FOB for short!"

"That's what I said," said Sister. "We're gonna raise money by going to Actual Factual's friends and begging for it."

• Chapter 9 •

Never Mind the Chickens

The scouts were moving along the same road they had traveled earlier on the way to their clubhouse. On this trip, they were headed for Farmer Ben's. His house and barn lay just over the rise.

Farmer and Mrs. Ben were good friends of the professor's. They would be happy to help. So would Ben's neighbors, Widder McGrizz and Dr. Gert. Miss Mamie, whose riding academy was next to Ben's farm, would also want to help.

"Look at that," said Fred. "There's a rooster on our clubhouse roof!"

"And chickens all around!" said Sister.

"Never mind the chickens," said Brother. "Look who's coming."

"It's Ralph," said Lizzy. Sure enough, it was. But it wasn't the shuffling, hangdog Ralph they had seen earlier. Not only did he have a spring in his step, a glint in his eye, and his stick a-twirl, but it looked like he was singing.

"Well," said Sister, "I guess we don't have to worry about him anymore."

"Wrong," said Brother. "When Ralph's feeling that good, it's time to *start* worrying. I don't think he's seen us. Let's duck behind these bushes. Maybe we can figure out what he's up to."

Ralph was indeed singing. If the scouts had been a little closer, this is what they would have heard:

Ralph Ripoff
is my name.
Termite insurance
is my game.
So whether your house
is oak or pine,
just sign here
on the dotted line.

Whether your house
is ash or cherry,
you better sign up
in a hurry.
Whether it's logs or boards
or railroad ties,
it could disappear
before your eyes!
So sign with Ralph.
Be a winner.
Or your house could be
a termite's dinner!
If your home sweet home
is made of wood,
you need Ralph because
only Ralph knows wood so good.
Only Ralph knows wood so good!

The way it worked out, all the scouts heard was the tail end of Ralph's song. When he disappeared around the bend, they came out from behind the bushes.

"'If your home sweet home is made of wood, you need Ralph because only Ralph knows wood so good!'" said Fred. "Now, what do you suppose *that* means?"

"Whatever it means," said Brother, "we can't worry about it right now. Come on! We've got money to raise!" Farmer Ben's house and barn were just ahead. They were both made of wood, of course.

• Chapter 10 •

Insurance by Ralph

"We'd sure like to help," said Farmer Ben. "The professor's our friend. But we're plumb out of cash money."

"That's right," said Mrs. Ben. "We just put all the cash we could find into termite insurance."

"Termite insurance?" said Brother.

"That's right," said Ben. "And we were lucky to get it."

"But there've never been any termites around here," said Fred.

"There are now," said Ben. "The Tasmanian termite! It's sweepin' up from the south. Layin' waste to whole towns!"

"Them critters was fixin' to eat us out of house and home," said Mrs. Ben. "Just look over there." The scouts looked. The corner of the house was eaten away. Sawdust was piled up all around.

"It was a fearsome sight to see," said Ben. "Throwed up sawdust like a snowblower throws snow." The scouts remembered the tail end of Ralph's song.

"I cooled 'em off with bug juice," said Mrs. Ben. "But it was a near thing. Now, of course, we've got termite insurance."

"By any chance was it Ralph Ripoff who sold you this insurance?" asked Brother.

"That's the funny part," said Ben. "Most times I wouldn't trust Ralph as far as I could throw him. But he sure saved our bacon this time around."

"And our house and barn," said Mrs.

Ben. "We've got an official insurance policy and everything. Here it is."

The Bear Scouts looked at the insurance policy. The cover said, "Insurance by Ralph. Termite Insurance a Specialty. Only Ralph knows wood so good!"

"Hmm," said Brother. "Have you spoken to any of your neighbors about this?"

"Sure thing," said Ben. "Seems them Tasmanian critters have hit this whole area. But Ralph helped 'em all out — the Widder McGrizz, Dr. Gert, Miss Mamie, everybody. Sorry we can't help the professor. Now, if you'll excuse me. I gotta bug-juice my foundations."

Suddenly it dawned on the scouts where Ralph was headed.

"Come on!" shouted Brother. "You saw Ralph! He was loaded for bear — his favorite sucker, Papa *Q*. Bear! Come on! *Run!*"

• Chapter 11 •

Like a Hot Knife Through Butter

By the time the Bears' tree house came into view, the Bear Scouts were puffing like four little engines that could. Ralph was there. But the scene wasn't quite what the scouts expected. Ralph was selling, all right. But Papa didn't seem to be buying. And Mama stood ready to step in if Papa weakened.

"Hold it!" said Brother. "Maybe Papa has finally learned to stand up to Ralph." The scouts kept out of sight and listened.

Papa was holding an insurance policy

just like the one Ralph had sold Farmer Ben.

"Good-looking policy, Ralph!" said Papa. "Nice curlicues."

"It's better than good-looking," said Ralph. "It's a first-class triple-A policy. Fully guaranteed to protect you against loss from termite damage."

"With all respect, Ralph," said Papa, "termites really don't amount to much around here."

"Why, bless your soul, my dear friend," said Ralph. "I'm not talking about *local* termites. I'm talking about the *Tasmanian termite.* They're sweeping up from the south. Leveling great forests. Laying waste to whole cities and towns!"

"You've fooled me many times," said Papa. "But I've learned my lesson. You're not going to fool me this time." Mama patted Papa on the back.

"You tell him, Papa!" whispered Sister from the scouts' hiding place.

"At least check with Farmer Ben and his neighbors," said Ralph. "They've seen the Tasmanian termite's deadly work."

"You don't understand, Ralph," said Papa. "This tree house of ours is *oak*. Those folks' houses are made of lesser woods. Why, the mighty oak . . ."

"*Oak?* Did you say *oak*?" said Ralph,

snatching the insurance policy away from Papa. "I couldn't *possibly* sell you termite insurance. Not for love or money. If you'll excuse me, I must be on my way." He tipped his hat to Mama.

"Er — why not?" asked Papa.

"Why not? Why not?" said Ralph as he moved toward the front gate. "Because, my friend, the Tasmanian termite *loves* oak. Goes through it like a hot knife through butter!"

"Oh," said Papa. Ralph headed down the road. As he did so, he reached inside his jacket and took out a tin box.

"Okay, Woody," said Ralph under his breath. "Do your thing. Go after the fence and the picnic table for starters." He opened the box and played out the fine nylon fishing line as Woody scurried through the grass.

"That Ralph," said Papa. "He's really

something. He almost had me convinced."

"I'm proud of you, dear," said Mama.

The scouts came out of their hiding place. "We're proud of you, too," said Sister. At that moment, they were all startled by what sounded like a buzz saw. As they turned toward the sound, they saw a whole section of fence turn into sawdust before their very eyes. After that, a picnic table.

"*HEL-L-LP!*" cried Papa. "The Tasmanian termite! Wait, Ralph! Wait! Please!" He ran after Ralph waving his wallet. "Mama!" he called. "Get the extra money out of the sugar bowl!"

"No, Papa! No!" cried Brother. "It's some kind of a trick!"

"What seems to be the trouble, my friend?" said Ralph when Papa caught up.

"The insurance! I'll buy it!" cried Papa. "Here's the money! And Mama's coming with more!"

"Well, I don't know," said Ralph. "What with your house being oak and all."

"Please, Ralph! *Please!*" cried Papa.

"Well . . . since it's you," said Ralph. "I'll let you have the insurance. Just sign right here." Papa signed with a shaking hand. Ralph pocketed the money and tipped his hat again. "It's been a pleasure doing business with you," he said. As he headed down the road, he reeled in the long nylon line and was about to put Woody back in the tin box.

"I know you are my friend," said Woody, "and I don't like to say this. But I don't think what you're doing is quite honest."

"Who asked you, sawdust breath?" said Ralph. "Now get back in your box, you disgusting little freak." He closed the box and put it back inside his jacket.

"Ralph! Ralph!" came Woody's muffled cry. "I thought you were my friend!"

"With friends like me, partner," said Ralph, "you don't need enemies."

Back at the tree house, the scouts were staring at the remains of the fence and the picnic table. "I saw it with my own eyes!" said Fred. "But I still don't believe it!"

"Come on!" said Brother.

"Where are we going?" said Lizzy.

"We're going to follow Ralph!" he said.

• Chapter 12 •

Help! I'm Being Kept Prisoner in Ralph's Mailbox!

Lizzy took the lead as the scouts followed Ralph into the woods. "Hold it!" she said, suddenly. "I hear something."

"If you mean that squawking," said Sister, "it's Ralph's pet parrot."

"Not the parrot," said Lizzy. "I hear voices, and it's not just Ralph."

"Then we'd better leave the path to be safe," said Brother. "We'll sneak up on the houseboat through the woods. Ralph might have a whole *gang* of crooks."

The scouts were in for a surprise when they reached the river. There was a gang, all right. But they weren't crooks. They were carpenters, painters, and mechanics fixing up Ralph's old houseboat. Even Ralph was working. He was putting up a big fancy sign that said "Ralph's Gamblerama."

"It's Ralph's old dream of turning his houseboat into a gambling ship," said Brother.

"Don't you mean 'nightmare'?" said Fred. "It'll be a license to steal!"

"He must have come into a lot of money," said Sister.

"Of course he has," said Brother. "A lot of Farmer Ben, Widder McGrizz, Dr. Gert, Miss Mamie, *and* Papa and Mama's money! Some of that money would have gone to Friends of the Bearsonian. So we've got to get it back!"

"How?" said Fred. "We don't have a clue

how Ralph's termite insurance swindle works."

"And we're not going to *get* any clues unless we get a lot closer," said Brother.

The scouts inched along until they were near the gangplank. There was so much going on that no one noticed them. The carpenters and the mechanics were hammering. Ralph was shouting orders, and Squawk was squawking. With all that noise, it was a wonder the scouts heard Woody's muffled cry.

"Help!" he cried. "I'm being kept prisoner in Ralph's mailbox!" Lizzy opened the mailbox a crack and looked in. It was a good thing she saw Woody first. Nature lover that she was, Lizzy wasn't nervous about crawly things. She turned to her fellow scouts.

"You know those mutation things the professor was telling us about? Well, there's a giant one in this mailbox. It's a termite as big as a kitten — and it talks!"

• Chapter 13 •

A Shower of Green

Woody was weak from hunger. So the scouts took him back into the woods. They brought him some twigs and branches. The buzz-saw sound effect and flying sawdust was all it took to show the scouts how Ralph's swindle worked.

Woody told the scouts how Ralph had befriended him. "He said we'd be partners," said Woody. "We were partners, all right — *partners in crime!* I'm so ashamed. Is there anything I can do to make up for my foolishness?"

"There just may be," said Brother. He told Woody what he had in mind. "Do you think you have the stomach for it?" he asked.

"Just try me," said Woody. As the Bear

Scouts approached the gangplank, Woody sneaked onto the houseboat and hid in the shadows.

"Well, if it isn't my favorite cubs, Scouts Brother, Sister, Fred, and Lizzy!" said Ralph. "You're welcome to come aboard!"

"This isn't a social visit, Ralph," said Brother. "We're here to get that crooked termite insurance money back!"

"You wound me deeply," said Ralph. "As for that money — I swindled it — er, earned it fair and square. And if you think . . ."

Woody didn't even wait for the signal. He popped out of the shadows and went to work on the houseboat. First, the railing disappeared in a cloud of sawdust. Then, the gangplank.

"Stop! Stop!" cried Ralph. "Can't we talk about this?" It wasn't until Woody went to work on Ralph's fancy new sign that he rushed below and came back with a huge basket of money. "Please! Not my sign!" He flung the money into the air. There was a shower of green. Woody and the scouts quickly gathered it up and disappeared into the woods.

"And after all I did for you!" shouted Ralph. "You . . . you . . . you *termite*!"

• Chapter 14 •
The Grand Reopening!

The grand reopening of the Bearsonian
did the Bear Scouts and the professor
proud. Grizzly Gus and his cleanup crew
made the old building shine. Mrs. Ben,
who was taking care of the coatroom, had
to send Farmer Ben for more coat hangers. The souvenir shop was selling everything from T-shirts that said, "I WAS AT THE
GRAND REOPENING OF THE BEARSONIAN" to
plastic dinosaur key rings. And, best of all,
every visitor got a special box of "Sawdust
by Woody."

Oh, yes. Woody was there. He was, in fact, the star of the show. Billed as "Woody, the Teenage Mutant Ninja Termite," he did demonstrations every hour on the hour. He would bow to a log like a karate master. But then, instead of breaking it in two with a karate chop, he ate it. As you might guess, he was a sensation.

But the grand reopening of the Bearsonian wasn't all glitz and show. There was plenty of solid science, too. The giant fruit fly models that Actual Factual had built out of balsa wood made the idea of mutation so clear that even Squire Grizzly understood it.

And Actual Factual had taped some push-button minilectures that explained modern dinosaur theory.

BCEC (Bear Country Electric Company) donated a huge lightning machine to the Hall of Energy.

Everybody who was anybody was there, including Scout Leader Jane. She was coming in just as the Bear Scouts were about to leave. The scouts started to make excuses about not deciding on their next merit badge. But Jane stopped them.

"Don't worry about it," she said. "There's more to life than merit badges. There's helping a great friend like Professor Actual Factual, for example!"

"I can't thank you enough for what you've done," said the professor.

"You're welcome," said Brother. "But we'd better be going. We've sort of let things slide at the clubhouse."

• Chapter 15 •

Let's Not and Say We Did

Had they ever! The Bear Scouts' chicken coop clubhouse may have been a secret, but it wasn't a secret from the chickens. They had just about taken it over. It was a mess.

"I guess it's time for the Grand Re-cleaning of the Bear Scouts' Clubhouse," said Brother. It wasn't easy. But after a lot of "shooing" and a lot of hard dirty work, the clubhouse was almost back to normal.

Breathing hard, the scouts collapsed onto chairs and the chicken roost they had fixed up with boards.

"Don't you think it's time to do our slogan?" said Fred.

"Let's not and say we did," said Brother.

So there they sat, tired, proud, and happy — and just a little bit smelly.

• About the Authors •

Stan and Jan Berenstain have been writing and illustrating books about bears for more than thirty years. Their very first book about the Bear Scout characters was published in 1967. Through the years the Bear Scouts have done their best to defend the weak, catch the crooked, joust against the unjust, and rally against rottenness of all kinds. In fact, the scouts have done such a great job of living up to the Bear Scout Oath, the authors say, that "they deserve a series of their own." Stan and Jan Berenstain live in Bucks County, Pennsylvania. They have two sons, Michael and Leo, and four grandchildren. Michael is an artist, and Leo is a writer. Michael did the pictures in this book.

Don't miss

THE Berenstain BEAR SCOUTS

and the
Coughing Catfish

"Can I give you a lift home?" said Gramps to the other scouts as Lizzy scampered ahead. "Got my pickup truck. But, say, you never did tell me what you're doing down by the lake."

"Thanks. We could use a lift," said Brother. "We're thinking of going for the Scuba-diving Merit Badge. So we're just down here checking things out."

That's when Brother was interrupted by someone screaming. "Help! Help! Come quick!" It was Lizzy. But she was nowhere in sight. She had been going toward shore, so there was no deepwater danger. Besides, Lizzy was a great swimmer.

The scouts rushed along the pier. When they got to where Lizzy had seen the minnows, they clambered down off the pier.

"Wait for me! Wait for me!" cried Gramps, who would have had a hard time keeping up even without the fishing gear. When he reached the spot and looked down, he was speechless. It wasn't because he was out of breath. It was because of what he saw. There, down in the shallows, with the foam cups and fry trays washing around their ankles, were the scouts. They were huddled around something so shocking that Gramps couldn't believe his eyes.

It was a fish. A huge catfish. A huge coughing catfish.

There's something fishy beneath the surface of Lake Grizzly....

THE Berenstain®
BEAR
SCOUTS
and the
COUGHING
CATFISH

by Stan & Jan Berenstain

Poor old Jake. He's the King of the Catfish — and he's coughing up a storm! It seems that Jake's lake has some serious pollution problems — and it's worse than just Styrofoam cups and plastic wrap. Can the Bear Scouts clean up Lake Grizzly and save the coughing catfish?

Coming in June

BBRCC1195

THE Berenstain BEAR® SCOUTS
by Stan & Jan Berenstain

Don't miss the Berenstain Bear Scouts' other exciting adventures!

Join Scouts Brother, Sister, Fred, and Lizzy as they defend the weak, catch the crooked, joust against the unjust, and rally against rottenness of all kinds!

☐ BBF60383-3	The Berenstain Bear Scouts and the Coughing Catfish	$2.99
☐ BBF60380-9	The Berenstain Bear Scouts and the Humongous Pumpkin	$2.99
☐ BBF60384-1	The Berenstain Bear Scouts and the Terrible Talking Termite	$2.99
☐ BBF60379-5	The Berenstain Bear Scouts in Giant Bat Cave	$2.99
☐ BBF60381-7	The Berenstain Bear Scouts Meet Bigpaw	$2.99
☐ BBF60382-5	The Berenstain Bear Scouts Save That Backscratcher	$2.99

© 1995 Berenstain Enterprises, Inc.

Available wherever you buy books or use this order form.

- -

Send orders to:
Scholastic Inc., P.O. Box 7502, 2931 East McCarty Street, Jefferson City, MO 65102-7502

Please send me the books I have checked above. I am enclosing $_____ (please add $2.00 to cover shipping and handling). Send check or money order — no cash or C.O.D.s please.

Name_____ Birthdate___ / ___ / ___
                                                              M   D   Y

Address_____

City_____ State_____ Zip_____